HERE COME THE TROLLS!

Here Come the Trolls!

RON BUTLIN

ILLUSTRATED BY JAMES HUTCHESON

The house where we live has
so many holes,
it leaks like a sieve and is
cram-full of trolls!

Through gaps in the roof
we didn't repair,
through cracks in the walls
we pretend aren't there...

...the trolls have come creeping
while we were all sleeping.

A TROLL'S HOUSE?...

Trolls on your chair, trolls in your bed –
is anything worse than a troll on your head?

Trolls, trolls,
  All gloom and frown,
Trolls, trolls,
  Getting us down.

Trolls in your eyes,
        a troll up your nose!
Ickly, tickly ...

Tchoo!

Out it goes!

We've too many holes,
Too many trolls,
Nose-dripping, fart-ripping,
Boot-clumping trolls.

BOOT-CLUMPERS

They're crowding us out
   (trolls hate being lonely),
five hundred, a thousand –
   standing room only!

So let's do some magic,
   just me and just you.
Let's clear out these trolls!
   Here's what we'll do . . .

On tip-toes, pretend
    we're reaching up high,
to turn on the rain . . .
Turn on the rain?

Yes!

And I'll tell you why.

Grubby trolls, greasy,
    all grungy and mean,
their outsides sick-queasy,
    their insides puke-green!
All scowl-mouthed and
    foul-mouthed,
trolls HATE being clean!

Now imagine a raindrop,
    another, and more –
Imagine the raindrops starting
    to pour . . .

Hear that first *thwack*
on our roof? That *smack!*
That thunder-loud crack
of a raindrop attack?

And soon all around
there's a *pit-patter* sound,
a dripping . . . a dribbling,
that trickles and rushes . . .
splashes and splishes and sploshes
and gushes . . .

... spatters our roof
till it floods through the holes
like we're running a bath –
a bath for the trolls!

A waterfall roars from the top
of the stairs!
Tables and chairs are dancing
in pairs!

There's a lake in the kitchen,
a pond in the hall,
a corridor river swirls
up the wall!

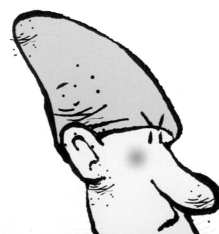

Trolls start to panic!
It's driving them manic!
They tremble and twirl,
their hair starts to curl!

All temper and tears,
    fists stuffed in ears,
they stamp on the ground,
    they twist themselves round.

Now imagine a whirlpool
    swirlpool sound . . .
going *swish-sweepy, wish-sleepy,*
    round and around . . .

A slow-turn, slow-churn
    will make the trolls feel
the whirlpool is *REAL!*

Imagine it *whirl* – imagine it *swirl*
faster and faster – an all-troll disaster!

Trolls start to frazzle, trolls start to *fizz.*

Its spin and its *whizz* wets a shoe, wets a toe
as troll number one is pulled in the flow . . .

Five trolls, now fifty are starting to go round and around . . .

A hundred, two hundred, up to their knees . . .
to their hips . . .
to their chests . . .
to their chins . . .
to their lips . . .

Then the whirlpool *GRIPS!*

And the last thing they hear
is its *gloorp* and its *slurp*
as it swallows them down,
with a watery . . .

BURP!

Trolls, trolls,
  They didn't stay long.
Trolls, trolls,
  Now they're all gone!

But wait . . . a troll!
Climbing the stair.
Two more in the sink –
they shouldn't be there!

The closer you look,
the more you will find –
drippy-wet, slippy-wet
trolls left behind

They're hiding from you
and hiding from me.
Look close – how many trolls
can you see?

Open the windows!
Fling wide the doors!

Stand clear, while a tidal wave
gathers and roars,
till every last troll is swept
off his feet,
out of the house and
into the street...

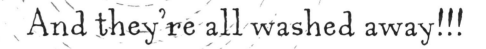

And they're all washed away!!!

HIP-HIP-HOORAY!

The magic we've done
    was troll-loads of fun.
So switch off the whirlpool,
    turn off the rain –
no trolls in the house;
    it's *ours* again!

Trolls, trolls,
    They tried to attack!
Trolls, trolls,
    We don't want them back!

Get hammers and nails,
    paintpots and pails,
chisels and saws!
    We need them because

we'll mend all the holes
    in the walls and the roof,
to fix up our house . . .

and make it
Troll-proof!

You've met all the trolls . . .
. . . and said, 'How d'you do?'

Did you catch sight
of girl-troll Goo?
of thick, clumping boots?
a troll who can swim?
a troll called Fart-Fart –
did you spot him?

See the sun smiling high
in the sky –
can *you* tell me why?

RON BUTLIN's award-winning poetry and novels have been widely translated. He has edited anthologies written by children, judged children's competitions and regularly gives writing workshops in schools. From 2008 to 2014 he was Edinburgh's Poet Laureate.

JAMES HUTCHESON is an award-winning illustrator, book designer and musician. He has worked with Ron on many other titles, including the recent *Magicians of Scotland*. They also performed together as part of *The Lost Poets Show* during three runs at the Edinburgh Festival Fringe.

First published in 2015 by
BC Books, an imprint of
Birlinn Limited
West Newington House
10 Newington Road
Edinburgh
EH9 1QS

www.birlinn.co.uk

ISBN: 978 1 78027 295 5

British Library Cataloguing-in-Publication Data
A catalogue record for this book is available from the British Library

Designed and typeset in MVB Aunt Mildred by James Hutcheson
Printed and bound in Latvia by Livonia

FREE AUDIOBOOK AVAILABLE!

We are giving away a free audio version of this book, as read by Ron Butlin.
To claim your free audio, all you have to do is email
BCBooks@Birlinn.co.uk
and say, 'Hello! Please send me my free audiobook of
Here Come the Trolls!'
We'll send you a link and a unique code for you to download and enjoy.